Wickiup Walkingstick

Story by Anne Macdonald
Illustrations by Elaine Blier

★★★★★★★★★
NORTHERN
LIGHTS BOOKS FOR CHILDREN
Red Deer College Press

Wickiup was a walkingstick, a
bug that looks like a twig from a tree.

He lived in a forest on the edge of the city. He saw lots of people riding bicycles, walking dogs. He saw many birds and small animals.

But no one could see Wickiup, he could hide so well among the plants. Hiding wasn't a game to Wickiup. It was his only protection from being eaten.

One afternoon some workers came to the forest. One man sprayed big orange X's on the dead trees to be cut down. Wickiup watched as the men drew nearer and nearer to his tree.

Suddenly one of the workers started up his chainsaw.

Rrroar!

It frightened Wickiup. He climbed to get away. Higher, faster, but …

Pssssst!

Wickiup felt a cool wet spray on his back. There was big orange X on the tree, and Wickiup was standing right in it.

He ran down the tree towards the pond to have a better look. His whole body was the colour of the sunset.

Then he saw something reflected in the water. Something getting nearer and nearer – a large, black bird looking for his dinner.

Swoooop!
The bird dived. Wickiup ducked.
The bird swooped down again and
again, trying to catch Wickiup.
Swoooop!
Over a log.
Swoooop!
And into a bush.

In the shadows Wickiup waited.
Finally the bird flew away, but Wickiup
was too terrified to move.
Being orange was dangerous!

When darkness came he crawled out of the bush. He tried to rub the paint off on the grass. It didn't work.

He tried to wash it off in a puddle. That didn't work either. He rolled in some mud and turned a nice shade of brown. That was better. But it wasn't green.

By morning the mud had dried. With every step it cracked and fell off in little pieces until Wickiup was all orange again.

Danger was all around. He could see birds searching for worms and insects for their breakfast.

Then he saw the workers again. This time they were spraying trees to mark a new pathway.

Psssst!

They sprayed a big X on a nearby tree. But this X was green. Wickiup knew what he must do.

They were coming his way. Quickly he backed down the tree and waited. Hungry birds flew low, lower, but he had to be patient.

Rrroar!

One of the workers started up his chainsaw, but Wickiup had to be patient.

Then the man with the spray can came right up to Wickiup's tree.

Pssssst!

Wickiup felt a cool spray on his back. There was a big green X on Wickiup's tree, and Wickiup was standing right in it!

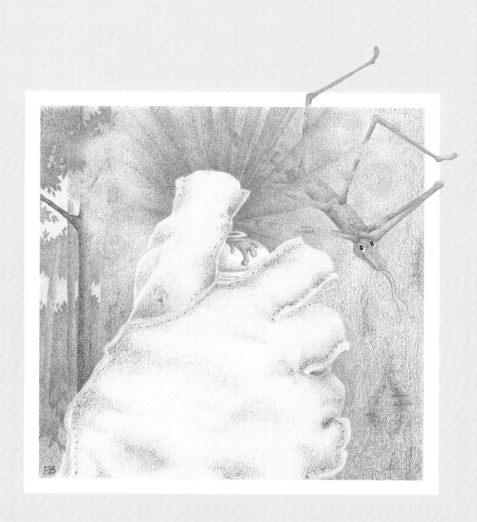

Clever Wickiup.

For Gerry –*E.B.*   For Alex, Jennie, Margaret, Graham –*A.M.*

Text Copyright © 1991 Anne Macdonald   Illustration Copyright © 1991 Elaine Blier
All rights reserved. No part of this book may be reproduced by any means, electronic or mechanical, including photography, recording, or any information storage and retrieval system, without permission in writing from the publisher.
Northern Lights Books for Children are published by
Red Deer College Press 56 Avenue & 32 Street Box 5005 Red Deer Alberta Canada T4N 5H5
Canadian Cataloguing in Publication Data
Macdonald, Anne
Wickiup walkingstick
(Northern Lights Books for Children)
ISBN 0-88995-063-6
I. Blier, Elaine, 1957- II. Title. III. Series
PS8575.D65W5 1991 jc813'.54 C90-091755-5
PZ7.M233Wi 1991
Acknowledgements
Edited for the Press by Tim Wynne-Jones. Designed by Elaine Blier. Printed and bound in Singapore by Kyodo Printing Co Pte.
The Publishers gratefully acknowledge the financial assistance of the Alberta Foundation for the Literary Arts, Alberta Culture and Multiculturalism, the Canada Council and Radio 7 CKRD.

LL
P
MAC

Macdonald, Anne
Wickiup Walkingstick

09/08	**DATE DUE**		